The Berenstain Bears
and the
EXCUSE NOTE

Every cub, if it's left up
to her or him,
can think of an excuse
to get out of gym.

A First Time Book®

The Berenstain Bears
and the
EXCUSE NOTE

Stan & Jan Berenstain

Random House New York

Copyright © 2001 by Berenstain Enterprises, Inc.
All rights reserved under International and Pan-American Copyright Conventions.
Published in the United States by Random House, Inc., New York, and
simultaneously in Canada by Random House of Canada Limited, Toronto.
www.randomhouse.com/kids   www.berenstainbears.com
Library of Congress Cataloging-in-Publication Data:
Berenstain, Stan, 1923–
The Berenstain Bears and the excuse note / by Stan & Jan Berenstain.
p.   cm. — (A first time book)
SUMMARY: Sister Bear dislikes gym class so much that she takes advantage of
a minor injury and sits on the sidelines instead.
ISBN 0-375-81125-7 (trade) — ISBN 0-375-91125-1 (lib. bdg.)
[1. Schools—Fiction.   2. Wounds and injuries—Fiction.   3. Bears—Fiction.]
I. Berenstain, Jan, 1923– II. Title. PZ7.B4483 Beet 2001 [E]—dc21 2001041667
Printed in the United States of America   September 2001 10 9 8
RANDOM HOUSE and colophon are registered trademarks of Random House, Inc.

Sister Bear liked school.
She liked almost everything about it.

She liked her classmates.

She liked her teacher.

She liked schoolwork, too.

She liked writing, although she had
a little trouble with some of the letters.

The Scardedy Kitten
Once there was a scardedy
Kitten. She was scarded of
everything. She was even
scarded of her own
shadow.
   One day she got tirred
of being scarded of her
own shadow.
   She said, "Shadow,
I'm not scarded of you
anymorre."
   And she wasn't.

Sisterr Bearr

Sister worked hard. After she got her *r*'s turned around, she got an A on one of her stories.

The Sad Rock (A)
Once there was
a sad rock. It
was sad because
it was a rock.
It wanted to
be a tree or a
flower or a
cloud. But the
tree got cut dow

But the rock just
kept on being a rock.
It wasn't sad anymore.
Sister Bear

Sister also liked reading. She liked it so much that she read whenever and wherever she could. She even took her school reader to bed with her right along with her teddy bear.

Sister liked numbers, too. You
could do so much with numbers!

You could count.

You could measure.

You could make
sure you got the
right change.

But there was one thing about school that
Sister didn't like. That thing was gym.

Sister had fun in the schoolyard.

She liked to run

and jump

and play games.

But gym wasn't fun and games. It was a sweaty, nasty nuisance. Sister wasn't the only one who groaned when Teacher Jane said it was time for gym.

Every day, Sister and her classmates had to push their tables and chairs out of the way to make room for

jumping jacks,

deep knee bends,

and the duck walk.

By the time they finished gym, Sister was hot, sweaty, and sore.

School would be so much nicer without dopey, *useless* gym, she thought as she helped push the tables and chairs back into place.

If only there were some way to get out of gym.

Then one day, as Sister was getting
off the school bus, she twisted her ankle.

The ankle hurt. Sister limped up their front steps. It didn't hurt *that* much, but it made her remember something. What she remembered was this: A while back, her friend Lizzy Bruin had broken her arm. The arm got better. But while it was hurt, Lizzy was excused from gym.

"Why are you limping, dear?" asked Mama Bear as Sister came in the door.

"I twisted my ankle getting off the bus," said Sister.

"Does it hurt a lot?" asked Mama.

"Yes," said Sister. "A *lot*."

"Let's put some ice on it to keep the swelling down," said Mama, "and we'll see how it feels in the morning."

"My ankle still hurts a lot," said Sister when she limped down to breakfast the next morning.

"You'll need a bandage on that ankle," said Mama.

"There's something else I'm going to need," said Sister.

"What's that?" asked Mama as she wrapped a support bandage around Sister's ankle.

"An excuse note," said Sister. "A note excusing me from gym."

This is the note that Mama wrote:

Dear Teacher Jane,
Please excuse Sister
from gym as she
has a sore ankle.
Thank you very much.
Sincerely,
Mama Bear

So when it was time for gym, Sister gave Teacher Jane the excuse note. Then she just sat and watched the rest of the class get hot, sweaty, and sore doing

jumping jacks,

deep knee bends,

and the duck walk.

Each day that she sat and watched, she thought how much nicer school was without gym. But as the days passed, there was just one problem: Her ankle wasn't sore anymore. Not the least bit.

When lunchtime came and a soccer ball bounced her way, Sister forgot she was supposed to have a sore ankle. She stood up and gave that ball a hard kick—*with the foot that was supposed to have a sore ankle!*

Then something strange happened. Someone sailed a paper airplane her way. It landed beside her "sore" ankle.

That someone was Teacher Jane! She had seen Sister kick the soccer ball. When Sister looked at the paper plane, she saw what it was. It was the excuse note.

"I guess your ankle is feeling better," said Teacher Jane.

"Much better, thank you," said Sister.

After school that day,
Sister took off the bandage.
She told Mama what had
happened at school.

"I see," said Mama.

"I hate that old gym!"
said Sister. "It makes me
all hot, sweaty, and sore—
and it's no use at all!"

Mama took Sister onto her lap, as she often did when she had something important to say. "It may make you hot, sweaty, and sore, my dear," she said, "but gym *is* useful—very useful, indeed. Just as writing, reading, and number work are good for your mind, gym is good for your body. It will make you stronger and healthier. It might even help you run faster and do other things better. But be that as it may, you may as well try to have fun because gym is part of school whether you like it or not."

Sister took Mama's advice. Once she stopped complaining about gym and did the best she could, it did get to be sort of fun.

In fact, Sister got so good at gym that Teacher Jane sometimes had her lead the class in jumping jacks,

deep knee bends,

and the duck walk.

And it *was* good for her body,
just as Mama said.

She *did* get to
be a faster runner

and a better jumper.

It also improved her soccer game.

But there was still one thing
she didn't like about school.
That thing was the duck walk.
　But then, nobody, but *nobody*,
likes the duck walk.